SPIKE
and the
SNOW DISCO

by

305

DEBORAH VAN DER BEEK

Illustrated by the author

HAMISH HAMILTON

LONDON

HAMISH HAMILTON LTD

Published by the Penguin Group
27 Wrights Lane, London w8 5tz, England
Penguin Books USA Inc., 375 Hudson Street, New York, New York 10014, USA
Penguin Books Australia Ltd, Ringwood, Victoria, Australia
Penguin Books Canada Ltd, 10 Alcorn Avenue, Toronto, Ontario, Canada m4v 3b2
Penguin Books (NZ) Ltd, 182–190 Wairau Road, Auckland 10, New Zealand

Penguin Books Ltd, Registered Offices: Harmondsworth, Middlesex, England

First published in Great Britain 1993 by Hamish Hamilton Ltd

1 3 5 7 9 10 8 6 4 2

British Library Cataloguing in Publication Data
CIP data for this book is available from the British Library

ISBN 0-241-13392-0

Set in 15pt Baskerville by Rowland Phototypesetting Ltd
Bury St Edmunds, Suffolk
Printed in Great Britain by BPCC Hazell Books Ltd
Member of BPCC Ltd, Aylesbury, Bucks.

Chapter One

Wheeeeeeee! Spike and Mole hurtled along the snowy track at what Spike said must be "at least a billion miles per hour". Mole, who liked to get things right, was about to argue the point, when they hit a hidden root and tumbled in a flurry of snow.

"It's definitely the best toboggan in the woods!" said Spike, sitting up and shaking snow from the bright pink spines on the top of his head.

This time Mole agreed with him.

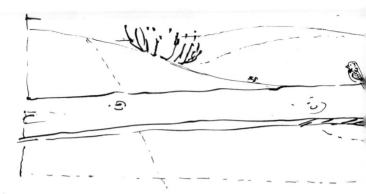

The toboggan was an old toast-rack, made of stainless steel, with most of the racks broken off; the two that were left provided useful paw-holds.

"In fact," added Spike, "I think we were travelling at supersonic speed. Didn't you hear that bang? I 'xpect that was us breaking the sound barrier."

Mole sighed. Really, sometimes his friend was a bit fanciful. "That," he explained patiently, "was us hitting a tree root."

Spike looked disappointed. "Well, jolly fast, anyway."

Just then, there was a slight noise behind them. It was Spike's sister Primrose. She was sitting in the beautiful blue toboggan their father

3

had carved from a coconut shell. It had a swan figurehead with red reins, and red cushions to match.

Spike and Mole did not have to move away quickly, for Primrose was travelling at a sedate pace: somehow, Mr Hedgehog had forgotten to smooth off the rough surface of the coconut shell.

Very slowly, Primrose came towards them, hit the same tree root and, as if in slow motion, sailed head first into the same pile of snow.

They watched the two little legs, helplessly beating the air.

"Er, can you yank her out?" Mole said.

Spike grinned. He knew why Mole didn't want to: ever since they'd

rescued Primrose from the clutches of
a nasty fox, she'd had a crush on
Mole.

"OK," said Spike. "Put in your
ear-plugs." They could hear muffled
cries from underground. Mole stuffed
his fingers in his ears: he knew
Primrose's shrieks of old.

Once rescued, Primrose insisted on being taken straight home. She was tucked up in bed with a hot-water bottle, and fed with tempting morsels suitable for a poor invalid.

The following morning, disaster struck. This was not because the snow had melted, or anything like that. On the contrary, more had fallen in the night: good packing snow, deeper than ever. No, this was something altogether different: the start of human school holidays.

All over the woods, young animals sat, clutching their toboggans, miserably listening to sounds of happy human children enjoying themselves.

By the end of the second day, Spike and Mole were desperate. (So were their parents.) They'd listened to their tapes until they were sick of them. (So were their parents.)

Suddenly, Mole sat up. "Got it!" he said.

"What?" asked Spike, but Mole wouldn't say. "Come on," he said.

Mystified, Spike followed.

Chapter Two

That morning, Mole had tunnelled through the snow to reach Spike's house. Now Spike followed him back along it. Half-way there, Mole turned and began carving a new tunnel up the hill.

Spike watched the flailing paws with admiration. The snow was soft, and Mole fairly flew along.

At the top of the hill, he popped out on to the surface for a moment. "Just taking a bearing," he said.

"We need a few airholes, anyway. I'll make sure they're out of sight to humans."

Now Mole began to dig straight down the hill again. This time he made sure the snow was packed down smoothly behind him. "Come on," he said. "Now we can get the toboggan."

"What, toboggan inside the tunnel?" Spike said. Mole nodded.

"Wow!" Spike gasped.

It was an amazing feeling whizzing along inside. It wasn't dark at all, but lit from all round by the whiteness of the snow.

They learnt to steer pretty accurately. If they didn't the sledge

climbed up the walls and they ended
upside-down. After a few runs, the
snow packed down hard, and they
got faster and faster.

"Shall I dig another?" Mole
suggested. "I'll make it a bit
different; put a few bends in."

Soon they had several more. Some
of their friends turned up and helped,
bringing tin lids and plastic tubs
with them, to sledge on.

They built tunnels with bends and tunnels with ramps where you flew through the air, landing with a bone-shaking jolt. They had straight tunnels for high-speed runs, and a rather nasty one where you ended up in a muddy ditch.

This last was not popular, until one night the weather turned colder, and the water in the ditch froze. Then it became the best of the lot: you sped down the run, and hit the ice, where you whirled about completely out of control. They called this the Dodgem Rink.

For a whole week, the human children played and sledged in the snowy wood, never dreaming that below its smooth surface young

animals were doing exactly the same. By now there was a maze of tunnels that writhed and twisted over, under and round about each other like a knot of tangled knitting.

Spike and Mole, who had started the whole thing, knew the maze as well as they knew the wood above it. Others were not so lucky, and many a young vole or hedgehog was late for dinner that week. As for the parents, they found it quite impossible.

Chapter Three

At last the children went back to
school, and the animals were able to
come out to explore and scavenge.
And what a mess had been left!

"I bags this can!"

"Wow, a balloon!"

"Any crisps left in there?" said
Mole, but Spike wasn't listening.

"What's that?" he said, pointing.
Mole saw a line of pressed down
snow that snaked off between the
trees. As they followed it along, the

15

track became larger and larger.
What could it be?

"There!" Spike said. Mole looked,
and gasped. Perched on the bank of
the stream was the largest snowball
they had ever seen. Without another
word, they raced towards it.

"It's gi-normous!" Spike said, as
they gazed up in admiration.

Mole reached out an experimental
paw and scratched the surface: it was
quite hard.

"Do you think you could get inside
it?" Spike asked. "Maybe we could

hollow a room out?"

"Dunno," Mole said. "I'll give it a try."

Inside the giant snowball the snow was softer, and soon the two friends were sitting out on top throwing snowballs at anyone who passed. Before long, a great battle was taking place.

Bit by bit, as they dug out the snow for more ammunition, the inside was hollowed out to make a very large room, and though the giant ball looked exactly the same from the outside, its frozen walls were as thin as Mole dared make them.

Long after everyone else had gone home, Spike and Mole sat listening

to pop music played at full blast. It
sounded good in the hollow chamber.

Suddenly, Spike jumped up
excitedly. "I know," he said. "We
could have a party in here. Right

inside the snowball. A snow disco!"

"Brilliant!" Mole said. His face
fell. "We'd have to clear it with the
parents though, otherwise they'd
never let us – and I'm late again!"

Spike groaned. "Aaagh! So am I –
we'll just have to wait for the right
moment."

Unfortunately, the right moment was some time in arriving. Suppose the weather changed, and the ball melted before they had a chance for a party?

Saturday came round once more, and humans were in the wood again. In the Hedgehog house, Primrose's face wore a look of deep sadness. She looked awfully sweet like that, with the tears welling up and hanging on her lashes like tiny pearls.

"So I can't have my Saturday Sweets then?" Her voice was wobbly with emotion.

"No darling," said Mrs Hedgehog. "I don't know my way about those tunnels at all. I'm sure Spike would go if he were here, but he isn't, and the shops close in an hour. When the snow melts you can have extra sweets. That will be nice, won't it?"

Primrose burst into tears. "No it won't. Anyway, Spike said he wouldn't get them unless I paid him 3p, and my pocket money's only 3p. Ohohohaaaaaaoh . . . I want my sweeties naaaaooooow."

Grandma, who had been sitting in the corner, watching all this in grim silence, sprang to her feet. "Charge his own sister for going to the shops!

I always said that son of yours was no good. Never been the same since he turned his spines that disgusting pink colour!"

"Well, he said he *might* not anyway," muttered Primrose in a voice so small that no one heard.

"Coat on!" said Grandma. "I'm taking you myself. Now."

"But – " Mrs Hedgehog tried to protest. "There are so many tunnels. It'll be dark soon and – "

Grandma cut her short. "PAH!" was all she said.

Primrose turned and waved to her mother. She was all togged up in the pretty blue outfit Mrs Hedgehog had made to go with her toboggan. There was a smug gleam in her eye.

Spike tried to sneak into the house without anyone seeing him. Late again, and they still hadn't asked about the disco . . .

But his mother had heard.

"Oh, it's you," she said, disappointed.

Spike, who had been expecting quite another reaction, was surprised.

Mr Hedgehog came in. "Is it them? Oh, no."

"We're very worried," Mrs Hedgehog explained. "Grandma and Primrose went to the sweetshop hours ago."

"It shouldn't take them that long," Spike said. "They must have got lost."

"It's dark now," said Mr Hedgehog. "And getting very cold . . ."

Mrs Hedgehog thought of Primrose's new coat. It was pretty, but not very warm. And Grandma was old. Old people got cold very quickly. If they sat and fell asleep, they could die from exposure . . .

Mrs Hedgehog felt helpless. If they were lost, they could be anywhere.

"I'll go and find them," Spike said. "Only I'll need to take Mole with me."

Chapter Four

Mole sat with his head in his paws.

"Come on," said Spike urgently.

"No, we've got to think," Mole said. "If they were on their way to the shops, they'd have gone uphill for a while, then turned right, then – "

"They could have missed that first turn," Spike said. "It would have still felt right, because of the slope. Only they'd be taken much further along, by the farm – "

"The slurry heap!"

Both animals thought of it at the same time. They had tunnelled all over the wood, but they had had to keep away from the giant heap of gently steaming cow-slurry. It was too old to smell much any more, but it gave off enough heat to make the tunnels nearby very dangerous indeed.

Spike's eye lit on a pile of yoghurt-pot lids, used by Mole's brothers and sisters as toboggans. After a moment's thought, he picked up four, and tucked them under his arm.

The two friends raced rapidly through the tunnels.

"Left here," said Mole.

A couple of times they missed a

turning, and had to retrace their steps.

"We must be getting near the farm now," said Spike.

"No, it's a bit further yet," Mole replied. He popped his head out of an airhole. It was pitch black outside. "Hang on a minute. Can you hear something?"

Spike listened. Nothing. Then it came again. Very faint and far off –

"O come into the garden
Ma-ud . . ."

The voice trailed away. Then
started up once more.

"Grandma!" said Spike. But it
didn't sound like the Grandma he
knew: it sounded very thin and weak.

The sound didn't come again.

They tried to locate where it had
come from, and moved in that
direction.

"Grandmaaa?" called Spike.
"Primrose?"

The noise echoed along the icy
walls of the tunnel. They waited with
ears strained. There was no reply.
All they could hear was an odd
sighing, creaking sound.

The snow had turned quite slushy.

The floor was littered with rusty tin lids: toboggans that had been grounded. They must be very near the slurry heap now.

"Up!" Mole shouted suddenly. "We've got to get out of here." He grabbed the astonished Spike and pulled him upward, scrabbling furiously through the roof of the tunnel and out into the open air.

They could see the large shape of the slurry heap, rising up beside them. "That creaking noise, it's the tunnel collapsing!"

All around them now, they could hear muffled rumblings and clickings, with a watery note coming in somewhere too.

"Primrose and Grandma!" cried Spike. "How can we find them now?"

Mole didn't say so, but he thought: it'll have to be soon. To Spike he said, "I can't walk properly here, I keep sinking in."

Just then Spike remembered the lids he had tucked under his arm. Quickly, he made two slits in each, and slipped them on his feet. "Snow-shoes," he said, flinging two at Mole. Mole put them on.

"Now all we need is a couple of sticks: it's what sheep farmers use, when they are searching for sheep buried in the snow."

Finding sticks was no problem in a wood. Spike and Mole walked easily

on their makeshift snow-shoes.

They moved round the slurry heap, gently poking their sticks where the snow had drifted deepest, and calling out at intervals. Spike got more and more worried: suppose they had got the wrong place altogether? Spike didn't like to think of it – it was a long time now since they had heard the voice, singing.

Suddenly, Mole gave a cry. "I think I've got them!"

He dug away the wet snow, and Spike helped.

It was the handbag they came to first. Then Grandma. She was quite still, and looked asleep. A moment later, a touch of blue: Primrose. But Primrose too seemed asleep. She was a funny grey colour.

Mole was rubbing Grandma's paws, hard.

Spike did the same with Primrose. They had to get the circulation going.

After what seemed like an awful long time, Grandma gave a groan, and muttered something that sounded like, "Get off!"

Mole carried on rubbing. A moment later, it happened again.

"Ruddy youngsters. All the same. Get OFF!" Grandma was on the mend.

But what of Primrose? Spike picked her up and shook her. Nothing happened at first, then there was a weedy little cry. She was alive!

Spike put her down and began to rub again. Mole helped. Before long, she was crying properly, and for once Spike didn't care.

When Primrose opened her eyes, the first thing she saw was Mole.

"Oh, Mole! You've saved my life again. Oh Mole, you're *so* clever!"

Primrose and Grandma were too weak to walk back, so Spike and Mole sat them on the plastic lids, and scooted them home. (Primrose shrieked horribly unless Mole did all the pushing.)

All four were greeted with delighted tears, given hot baths and sent to bed.

Mr and Mrs Hedgehog were very proud. As they tucked Spike in, Mrs Hedgehog said, "You were very brave, you know. We'd like to hold a party for you, to celebrate saving their lives. Would you like that?"

Spike immediately thought of the snow disco. "Oh, yes please!" he gasped.

And so it was decided.

Chapter Five

It was the day of the disco. Up until now, the weather had remained dull. That morning, however, for the first time since the snow fell, a winter sun shone clear and bright. The wood looked beautiful as Spike and Mole, laden with cassettes and equipment, made their way to the giant snowball.

Suddenly, Spike came to an abrupt halt.

"Look at the snowball!" he

gasped. Mole gasped too. The ball was still there, and as large as ever, but now it glowed with a strange unearthly light. It looked like a giant diamond, or crystal ball.

"What's happened?" said Spike in an awed whisper.

They approached slowly, almost expecting the thing to take off and disappear into space.

"I'm sure – I'm almost sure I can see through it," said Mole, frowning in the brightness.

Slowly they realized what had happened. The slight warmth of the sunshine had melted the surface of the hollowed-out snowball which had then frozen again, making the ball transparent. Sunlight turned and

36

twisted on tiny flaws in the ice, and it
sparkled in a thousand rainbow
colours.

"It's wonderful," breathed Spike.

Before long, several others had
turned up to admire and gape. Word
got around rapidly. Spike hoisted a
flag out at the top, to remind
everybody of the disco that night.

It was a party they would all
remember for a very long time.

Spike re-dyed the pink spines on the top of his head, and they gleamed and reflected on the shiny ice walls.

Mole's shirt was of such a violent mix of colours, you needed dark shades to look at it.

If any humans had walked through the wood that night, what would they have made of it? A luminous crystal orb, shooting out coloured lights on to the snowy surroundings, and belting rock music to the puzzled trees.

Whatever it might have looked like from the outside, however, there was no doubt that those within were enjoying themselves. When they were too hot with dancing, they flattened themselves against the walls of ice, or simply stuck out their tongues and drank in the coolness.

Spike looked round at all the happy faces, and felt pleased and proud to think that it was he and Mole who had made it happen. Mole caught his eye and grinned.

But good things don't last for ever, and eventually Mr Hedgehog and the other parents arrived to take them all home. Primrose, quite recovered from her adventure, was sitting on her father's shoulders. She had made Mr Hedgehog promise to wake her up and see just a little bit of the party. Her eyes were large with excitement, and she still wore her nightdress under her coat.

It was the last dance, and

Primrose wanted to join in. To
Mole's embarrassment, she *insisted* on
dancing with him. Everyone else
thought this was hilarious. "Whooo
hooo!" they yelled, and wolf-whistled
and cat-called.

Primrose loved all the attention,
making Mr Hedgehog think gloomily
of the day when Primrose would be
Spike's age: if Spike was bad,
Primrose was going to be dreadful!